BOXES
FOR KATJE

Candace Fleming

Pictures by
Stacey Dressen-McQueen

MELANIE KROUPA BOOKS

FARRAR, STRAUS AND GIROUX ◆ NEW YORK

To Mom, for sharing her life's stories
—C.F.

To Rob
—S.D.M.

Text copyright © 2003 by Candace Fleming
Illustrations copyright © 2003 by Stacey Dressen-McQueen
All rights reserved
Distributed in Canada by Douglas & McIntyre Publishing Group
Color separations by Chroma Graphics PTE Ltd.
Printed and bound in the United States of America by Berryville Graphics
Designed by Jennifer Browne
First edition, 2003
10 9 8 7
www.fsgkidsbooks.com

Library of Congress Cataloging-in-Publication Data
Fleming, Candace.
  Boxes for Katje / by Candace Fleming ; pictures by Stacey Dressen-McQueen.— 1st ed.
    p.   cm.
  Summary: After a young Dutch girl writes to her new American friend in thanks for the
care package sent after World War II, she begins to receive increasingly larger boxes.
  ISBN 0-374-30922-1
  [1. Generosity—Fiction.   2. World War, 1939–1945—Civilian relief—Fiction.
3. Netherlands—Fiction.]   I. Dressen-McQueen, Stacey, ill. II. Title.

PZ7.F59936 Bo 2003
[E]—dc21

                                                            2002020027

After the war, there was little left in the
tiny Dutch town of Olst. The townspeople lived
on cabbages and seed potatoes. They patched and
repatched their worn-thin clothing, and they went
without soap or milk, sugar or new shoes.

One spring morning, when the tulips bloomed thick and bright, Postman Kleinhoonte pedaled his bicycle down the cobbled street.

"Oh ho!" he whooped. "I have a box for Katje—a box from America!"

"America?" exclaimed Katje. "Who would send me a box from America?"

"The Children's Aid Society," replied the postman. "Children in America
are collecting and mailing many hard-to-find items to the children of
Holland. You, young miss, were lucky to get one."

Katje took the box. She rubbed her finger across the block letters that
spelled "U.S.A."

"The land of plenty," she whispered.

Katje's mama came to stand beside her. "Open it," she urged.

Peeling off the brown paper wrapping, Katje pushed back the flaps and pulled out—"A cake of soap!"

"What luxury," said Mama. "No more bathing with gritty, homemade stuff for you."

Katje pulled out the next item—"A pair of wool socks!"

"Now, that *is* luxury," said Postman Kleinhoonte.

"Holland has become a sockless country since the war."

He rolled up his pant leg to show his bare ankle.

Katje dipped into the box again. Out came—"Chocolate!"

Mama sniffed, then sighed. "I have not smelled chocolate in years."

Postman Kleinhoonte smacked his lips. "I have not *tasted* chocolate in years."

"Neither have I," added Katje. Her mouth watered as she remembered its creamy, rich sweetness. She could hardly wait to take a bite. Then she looked from Mama's smiling face to Postman Kleinhoonte's. And Katje made a decision.

Quick, before she could change her mind, she broke the bar into pieces and passed them around. For several moments the three savored the almost forgotten taste.

Then Postman Kleinhoonte pointed. "That box is not empty yet."
Katje reached in and pulled out a letter. It read:

Dear Dutch Friend,

I hope these gifts brighten your day.

Your American Friend,

Rosie Johnson
123 Elm Street
Mayfield, Indiana
U.S.A.

The postman nodded. "*Ja*. Rosie's box brightened my day."
"And mine," agreed Mama.
"I am going to tell her," decided Katje. "I am going to send a letter to Rosie."

Dear American Friend,
    Thank you for the soap and the socks, but most of all for the chocolate.
    Sugar is not found in Holland these days, so anything sweet is precious.
    My mother and Postman Kleinhoonte very much enjoyed it, too.

        Your Dutch friend,
    Katje Van Stegeran

Weeks passed and summer came, hot and bright.

The townspeople of Olst boiled cabbages, dug potatoes, and dreamed of meat and bread.

One morning, while Katje and her mama pulled up their tulips, rubbed off the stems, and sorted the bulbs into bags, Postman Kleinhoonte came pedaling down the street.

"She has another one!" he hollered. "Katje has another box from America!"

His shouts drew Mr. and Mrs. deLand and their five thin children from next door.

Everyone gathered around as Katje eagerly opened this second, bigger box.

"Johan, look!" shrieked Mrs. deLand when the flaps were pulled back.

"I am looking," gulped her husband, "but I am not believing my eyes."

From the box Katje pulled four bags of sugar and a letter from Rosie.

Dear Katje,

No sugar? Yikes!
That's so awful
Mother and I are
sending you some.
We included
some for your
postman, too.

Your friend,
Rosie

"Sugar, sugar, sugar," sang Postman Kleinhoonte. Grabbing the smallest deLand, he danced with the toddler to the word's sweet beat.

And Katje made a decision. "There is plenty to share," she said.

"Ach!" sobbed Mrs. deLand, dabbing away tears with the corner of her apron. "You are too kind! *Dank u*, Katje! Thank you!"

Then, as Postman Kleinhoonte sang, the children danced, and Mrs. deLand sniffled, Katje divided the sugar.

Later, she wrote to Rosie:

Dear Friend Rosie,
So many sweets!
How can I ever
thank you?
I shared the sugar
with our neighbors,
Mr. and Mrs. deLand.
They have five
children who are
skin and bone.
With so little food
in Holland, it is
hard to keep
anyone fed. Your
gift has surely
helped us.
Your friend,
Katje

Weeks passed, and autumn came, rainy and gray.

The townspeople of Olst picked the last of their cabbages and potatoes. They lined their old coats with newspaper to keep out the cold air. And they worried about the coming winter.

"How will we survive without good food or warm clothing?" they asked each other. "How will we live?"

Katje and her mama worried, too. But as always, they planted their tulip bulbs in the hardening ground, and looked forward to the day the tulips would bloom. They were brushing dirt from their knees when Postman Kleinhoonte came stumbling down the street.

"It is a big one!" he shouted. "So big I could not bring it on my bicycle! *Ja! Ja!* A big, heavy box from America!"

His excited shouts drew Dr. Bos
from his office and the widow
Gans from her yard. They drew
Miss Oosterveld, and Schoolmaster
deLeeuw, and all seven of
the deLands.

Everyone crowded around as Katje dug into this third, bigger box from America.

"*Wonder baar!*" shouted Dr. Bos, when he looked in the box. "Such generosity!"

There were cans of meat, boxes of powdered milk, bags of sugar, and a letter from Rosie.

Dear Katje,

Jeepens! You'll never guess. Mother told her friends about your last letter, and they told their friends, and our doorbell just kept ringing. "Send this to Katje," people kept saying. So we did.

Hope this puts some fat on those deLand kids.

Love,
Rosie

"Oh, it will! It will!" cried Mrs. deLand.

And Katje made another decision. "There is plenty to share," she said.

"Bless you!" cried Miss Oosterveld.

Amid kisses and hugs and heartfelt *dank u*'s Katje divided the food.

And later, she wrote to Rosie:

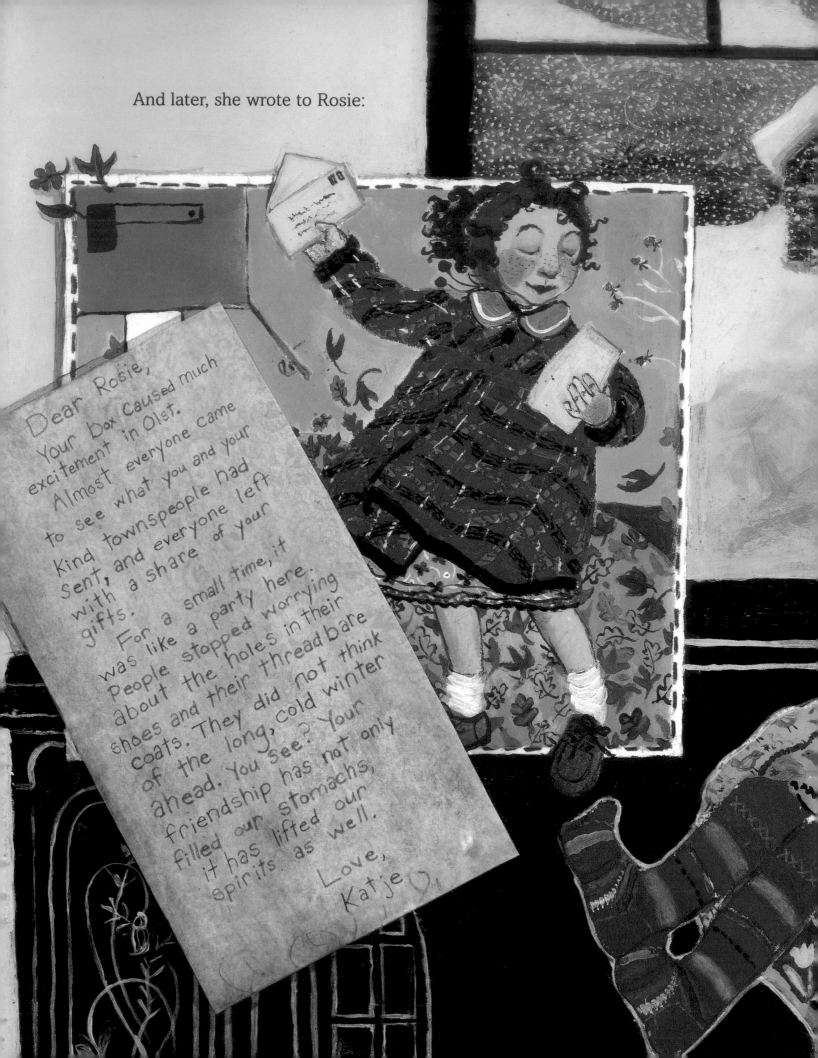

Dear Rosie,
Your box caused much excitement in Olst. Almost everyone came to see what you and your kind townspeople had sent, and everyone left with a share of your gifts.
For a small time, it was like a party here. People stopped worrying about the holes in their shoes and their threadbare coats. They did not think of the long, cold winter ahead. You see? Your friendship has not only filled our stomachs, it has lifted our spirits, as well.
Love,
Katje

Weeks passed, and winter roared in, snow-deep and bitter cold, the worst winter anyone could remember.

The townspeople of Olst layered whatever clothing they had. They huddled close to their small fires, ate sparingly from their almost empty cupboards, shivered, and prayed.

One dark morning, when Katje felt as frozen as the tulip bulbs buried beneath the snow, there came a pounding on her door.

She opened it to find Postman Kleinhoonte and the townspeople crowded into the yard.

THIS SIDE UP ↑

"What a delivery I have for you!" whooped
the postman. He pulled a sled, stacked high
with boxes, straight into the house.

"So many!" gasped Katje.

"*Ach*, but there are more!" cried the postman.
Squeezing his way through the crowd, he
returned with another box-stacked sled. And
another. And still another.

There was barely room for boxes and people
as Katje pushed back flaps and pulled out—coats,
mittens, socks and shoes, scarves, hats, and sweaters.

Cakes of soap! Chocolate bars!
And bags, cartons, and cans of food!

At the bottom of the very last box,
there was a letter from Rosie.

Dear Katje,

You won't believe what's happening here! Everyone, everywhere, wants to send a box to you. The school organized a canned food drive. The church organized a clothes drive. Even the local businesses added items to the boxes. We hope there's enough here for all your friends and neighbors.

Love,
Rosie

For several seconds the townspeople of Olst stood in speechless wonder.

Then Katje cried, "There is plenty to share!"

"Hooray!" Postman Kleinhoonte danced a jig in his new wool socks. Mrs. deLand wept while buttoning five warm coats. And Dr. Bos put down his cans to give the widow Gans a quick, joy-filled kiss.

Mama wrapped her arms around Katje. "You have brought us a miracle," she said.

"No," replied Katje. "Rosie did."

All winter long, the boxes kept coming. All winter long, the townspeople stayed warm and well fed. And all winter long, Katje wrote letters to her American friend, Rosie.

Slowly the snow melted, and the wind lost its bite. Each day more and more tulips poked their green tips through the soil, blooming into a sea of pink and yellow, purple and red.

One warm morning Katje said, "It would be nice to send a box to Rosie."

"*Ja,*" said Mama. "But what would you send?"

Katje smiled as she told her.

"It is a good idea," said Mama.

"Oh ho! I like it!" agreed Postman Kleinhoonte.

"We must do it," said the deLands.

"Together!" added Dr. Bos.

And so one sun-bright morning, Mr. Everett, the mailman, hurried down Elm Street. "I have a box for Rosie!" he announced. "A box from Holland!"

"Holland!" exclaimed Rosie. "What could it be?" Eagerly she ripped off the wrapping and pulled back the flaps.

"So many!" gasped her mother.

Then Rosie read the letter:

Dear Rosie,
We hope these tulip bulbs from Olst will brighten Mayfield's days.

Plant them in the fall and wait for a surprise in the spring.
Love,
Katje

A True Story about Boxes

This book is based on events that really happened. In May 1945, my mother sent a small box to Europe. Inside was a tube of toothpaste, a pair of socks, a bar of soap, and a note. The note, written in my mother's hard-to-read scrawl, sent good wishes and included her address.

Her box was one of thousands that poured into Europe from America that spring. Under the direction of charities such as the Children's Aid Society, Catholic Relief Services, and the American Red Cross, people all across the nation were packing badly needed items into boxes and mailing them to desperately needy Europeans.

After World War II, Europe stood in ruins, its buildings bombed, its roads and bridges damaged, its economy destroyed. Poverty spread and food was scarce. Still, Europeans managed to survive the spring, summer, and fall of 1945. But then winter arrived—the worst winter of the century—plunging temperatures below zero and, in some places, piling up thirty feet of snow. The frigid weather left many Europeans shivering in their homes, cold, hungry, and hopeless. In Holland, some people were so desperate they were forced to eat their own tulip bulbs.

My mother's box found its way to a Dutch family whose oldest daughter was named Katje. It was Katje's father who wrote back, asking if my mother could spare a box of powdered milk for the baby, or a bag of sugar, or perhaps a few cans of meat. The pressing needs of Katje's family tore at my mother's heart. What began with one woman and one small box grew into a churchwide effort to support Katje's family through the hard winter. Sugar, powdered milk, coats—all this and more traveled across the Atlantic in a steady flow from Indiana to Holland.

Katje's family survived. And when conditions in Holland began to improve, they sent a box to their American friends—a box of tulip bulbs, bulbs that my mother and others planted all over town.

I like to think those tulips are still blooming.